P9-DTU-412

JUL 2 1 1980

SEP 1 1982

AUG 1 4 1985

MAR 1 3 1989

AUG 8 1980

SEP 17 1982 FEB 2 0 1984

DEC 4 1987

APR 1 4 1989

SEP 1 7 1980

DEC 1 4 1982

AUG 2 0 1985

FEB 2 2 1988

AUG 8 1989

OCT 2 9 1989

OCT 1 6 1980

FEB 9 1983

SEP 5 1985

Mar. 16 1988

FEB 4 1990

Oct 30 1980

MAR 4 1983

NOV 9 1985

2-20-90

DEC 5 1980

MAR 1 9 1983

MAY 2 8 1986

APR 5 1988

FEB 9 1981

APR 1 9 1983

JUL 1 4 1986

APR 3 0 1988

MAR 1 5 1990

FEB 1 6 1981

JUL 7 1983

AUG 2 5 1986

MAR 3 1 1990

MAY 2 9 1981

JUL 2 0 1983

JUL 5 1988

OCT 2 8 1981

AUG 9 1983

SEP 2 7 1986

APR 3 0 1990

NOV 1 8 1981

JAN 2 1 1984

FEB 1 1 1987

SEP 1 2 1988

MAY 2 9 1990

NOV 2 8 1981

APR 1 4 1984

MAR 7 1987

NOV 4 1988

DEC 1 5 1981

APR 2 1987

MAR 2 9 1989

OCT 1 1 1990

JUN 7 1982

SEP 2 1 1984

APR 1 4 1987

MAY 2 4 1989

MAR 1 3 1990

OCT 2 7 1990

JUN 2 8 1982

APR 2 8 1987

AUG 1 6 1982

MAY 2 0 1983

JUN 2 4 1987

JUL 1 3 1987

JUL 2 9 1987

SEP 1 0 1987

OCT 3 0 1987

One-Eyed Jake

by Pat Hutchins

Greenwillow Books

A Division of William Morrow & Company, Inc.

New York

Library of Congress Cataloging in Publication Data   Hutchins, Pat (date)   One-eyed Jake.   Summary: A greedy pirate plunders one ship too many.   [1. Pirates—Fiction] I. Title. PZ7.H96165On [E]   78-18346   ISBN 0-688-80183-8   ISBN 0-688-84183-X

For Claire Louise Goundry

Once there was a pirate
called One-Eyed Jake.
He had a horrible face,
a terrible voice,
and an awful temper.

Nobody liked him.

The cook was terrified of him,

the bosun was frightened of him,

and Jim the cabin boy was scared of him.

One-Eyed Jake robbed every ship in sight.
He robbed the enormous passenger ships
of their treasures,
and dropped them into the hold.

He robbed the huge cargo boats of their cargo,
and tossed that into the hold.

He even robbed the little fishing boats of their catch
and shoved that into the hold, too.
And if anyone dared complain,
he threw him overboard.

One day the cook said,

"I'm tired of stealing for One-Eyed Jake.

I'd like to cook nice dinners

on an enormous passenger ship."

And the bosun said,

"I'm tired of stealing, too.

I'd like to steer a big cargo boat."

And Jim the cabin boy said,

"I don't like stealing, either.

I'd like to work on a little fishing boat,

and take the cat with me."

But they didn't dare complain to One-Eyed Jake,

in case he threw them overboard.

So they kept robbing and plundering

until the ship's hold was so full

that they had to pile the loot on the deck.

But still One-Eyed Jake wanted more.

He spotted an enormous passenger ship,
and robbed the passengers
of all their jewelry,
but the hold was so full,
and the loot so heavy,
that the boat started sinking.
"Ha-ha!" said the passengers.
"Your ship will sink with
the weight of the jewels!"

"Ha-ha, yourself!" said One-Eyed Jake,
and knowing that the cook
was heavier than the jewels,
he tossed him onto the passenger ship,
and sailed away.

Then he spied a big cargo boat,

and robbed the crew

of their cargo of peacock feathers,

but the hold was so full,

and the loot so heavy,

that the boat started sinking.

"Ho-ho!" said the crew.

"Your ship will sink with the weight

of the feathers!"

"Ho-ho, yourself!" said One-Eyed Jake,
and knowing that the bosun
was heavier than the feathers,
he threw him onto the cargo boat,
and sailed away.

Then he saw a little fishing boat,

and robbed the fishermen of their catch,

but the hold was so full,

and the loot so heavy,

that the boat started sinking.

"Hee-hee!" said the fishermen.

"Your ship will sink with the weight of the fish!"

"Hee-hee, yourself!" said One-Eyed Jake,

and knowing that Jim the cabin boy was

heavier than the fish,

he threw him onto the fishing boat.

But Jim, who was a clever lad, shouted,
"Here's the key to the cabin!"
And One-Eyed Jake,
who was not so clever,
caught it in his hand.

But the hold was so full,

and the loot so heavy,

that before anyone could say,

"Ha-ha!

Ho-ho!

Hee-hee! Your ship will sink with the weight of the key!"

...it had.

The cook was very happy cooking nice dinners
on the enormous passenger ship,
the bosun was very happy steering the huge cargo boat,
and Jim the cabin boy was very happy
working on the little fishing boat with the cat.
And One-Eyed Jake was never seen again.